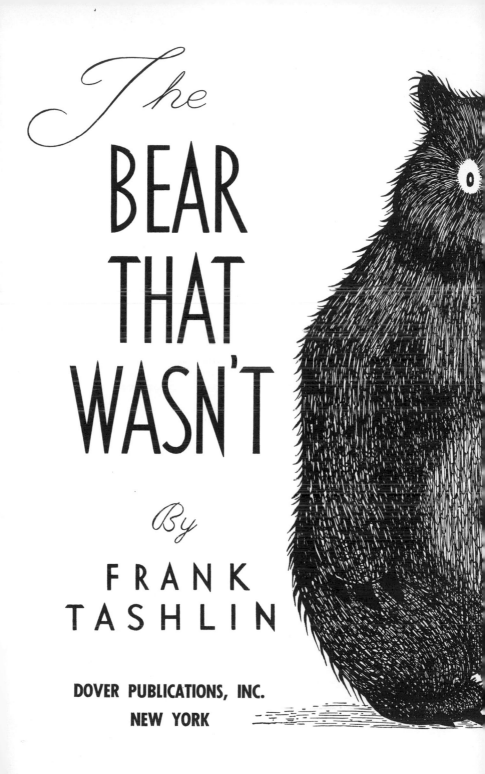

The
BEAR
THAT
WASN'T

By

FRANK
TASHLIN

DOVER PUBLICATIONS, INC.
NEW YORK

Published in Canada by General Publishing
Company, Ltd., 30 Lesmill Road, Don Mills,
Toronto, Ontario.
Published in the United Kingdom by Constable
and Company, Ltd., 10 Orange Street, London
WC 2.

This Dover edition, first published in 1962, is an
unabridged and unaltered republication of the work
originally published by E. P. Dutton & Co., Inc., in
1946.

Standard Book Number: 486-20939-3

Library of Congress Catalog Card Number: 62-4936

Manufactured in the United States of America
Dover Publications, Inc.
180 Varick Street
New York, N.Y. 10014

TO

PATRICIA ANNE

THE

LITTLE

GIRL

THAT

IS.

Once upon a time, in fact it was on a Tuesday, the Bear stood at the edge of a great forest and gazed up at the sky. Away up high, he saw a flock of geese flying south.

Then he gazed up at the trees of the forest. The leaves
had turned all yellow and brown and were falling
from the branches.

He knew when the geese flew south and the leaves fell
from the trees, that winter would soon be here and snow
would cover the forest. It was time to go into a cave
and hibernate.

And that was just what he did.

Not long afterward, in fact it was on a Wednesday, men came . . . lots of men, with charts and maps and surveying instruments. They charted and mapped and surveyed all over the place.

Then more men came, lots of men with steamshovels and saws and tractors and axes. They steamshoveled and sawed and tractored and **axed** all over the place.

They worked, **and** worked, and worked, **and** finally they
built a great, big, huge,

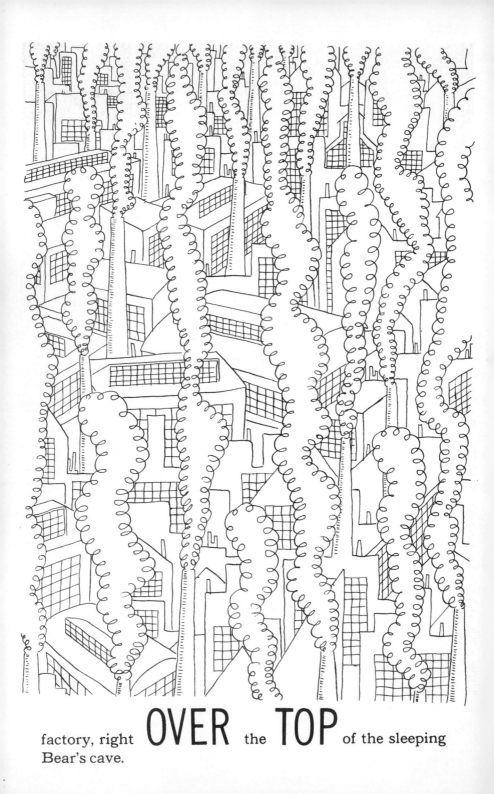

factory, right **OVER** the **TOP** of the sleeping Bear's cave.

The factory operated all through the cold winter.

And
then
it
was
SPRING
again

Deep down under one of the factory
buildings the Bear awoke. He
blinked his eyes and yawned.

Then he stood up sleepily and
looked around. It was very dark.
He could hardly see.

Then he saw a light in the distance.
"Oh, there's the entrance to the cave,"
he said, and yawned again.

He walked up the stairs
to the entrance

and stepped out into the bright
spring sunshine. His eyes were
only half opened, as he was still
very sleepy.

His eyes didn't stay half opened
long.

They suddenly POPPED
wide apart.
He looked straight ahead.

Where was the forest?
Where was the grass?
Where were the trees?
Where were the flowers?

WHAT HAD HAPPENED?

Where was he?

Things looked so strange. He didn't know
where he was.

But we do, don't we? We know that he was right in the
middle of the busy factory.

"I must be dreaming," he said.
"Of course that's it, I'm dreaming."
So he closed his eyes and
pinched himself.
Then he opened his eyes very
slowly and looked about. The big
buildings were still there. It wasn't
a dream. It was real.

Just then a man came out of a door.

"Hey, you get back to work," the man said. "I'm the *Foreman* and I'll report you for not working."

The Bear said, "I don't work here. I'm a Bear."

The Foreman laughed very loud.

HA HA HA

"That's a fine excuse for a man to keep from doing any work."

HA HA HA HA

"Saying he's a Bear."

HA HA

The Bear said, "But, I am a Bear."

The Foreman stopped laughing. He was very mad.

"Don't try to fool me," he said. "You're not a Bear. You're a silly man who needs a shave and wears a fur coat. I'm going to take you to the *General Manager*."

The Bear said, "No, you're mistaken. I am a Bear."

The General Manager was very mad, too.

He said, "You're not a Bear. You're a silly man who needs a shave and wears a fur coat. I'm going to take you to the *Third* Vice President."

The Bear said, "I'm sorry to hear you say that . . . You see, I am a Bear."

The Third Vice President was
even madder.

He got up out of his chair and said,
"You're not a Bear. You're a silly
man who needs a shave and wears
a fur coat. I'm going to take you
to the *Second* Vice President."

The Bear leaned over his desk and
said, "But that isn't true. I am
a Bear, just a plain, ordinary,
everyday Bear."

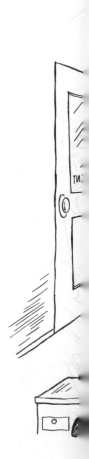

The Second Vice President was more than mad or madder. He was furious.

He pointed his finger at the Bear and said, "You're not a Bear. You're a silly man who needs a shave and wears a fur coat. I'm going to take you to the *First* Vice President."

"Who? Me?" the Bear asked. "How can you say that, when I am a Bear?"

The First Vice President yelled in rage.

He said, "You're not a Bear. You're a silly man who needs a shave and wears a fur coat. I'm going to take you to the *President*."

and the Foreman, have told me that already."

"Thank you for telling me," the President said. "I won't say it, but that's just what I think you are."

The Bear said, "I'm a Bear."

The President smiled and said,
"You can't be a Bear. Bears are only
in a zoo or a circus. They're never
inside a factory and that's where
you are; inside a factory. So how
can you be a Bear?"

The **Bear said**, "But I am a Bear."

The President said, "Not only are you a silly man who needs a shave and wears a fur coat, but you are also very stubborn. So I'm going to **prove** it to you, once and for all, that you are *not* a Bear."
The Bear said, "But I *am* a Bear."

AND

SO

THEY

ALL

GOT

INTO

THE

PRESIDENT'S

CAR

AND

DROVE

TO

THE

ZOO

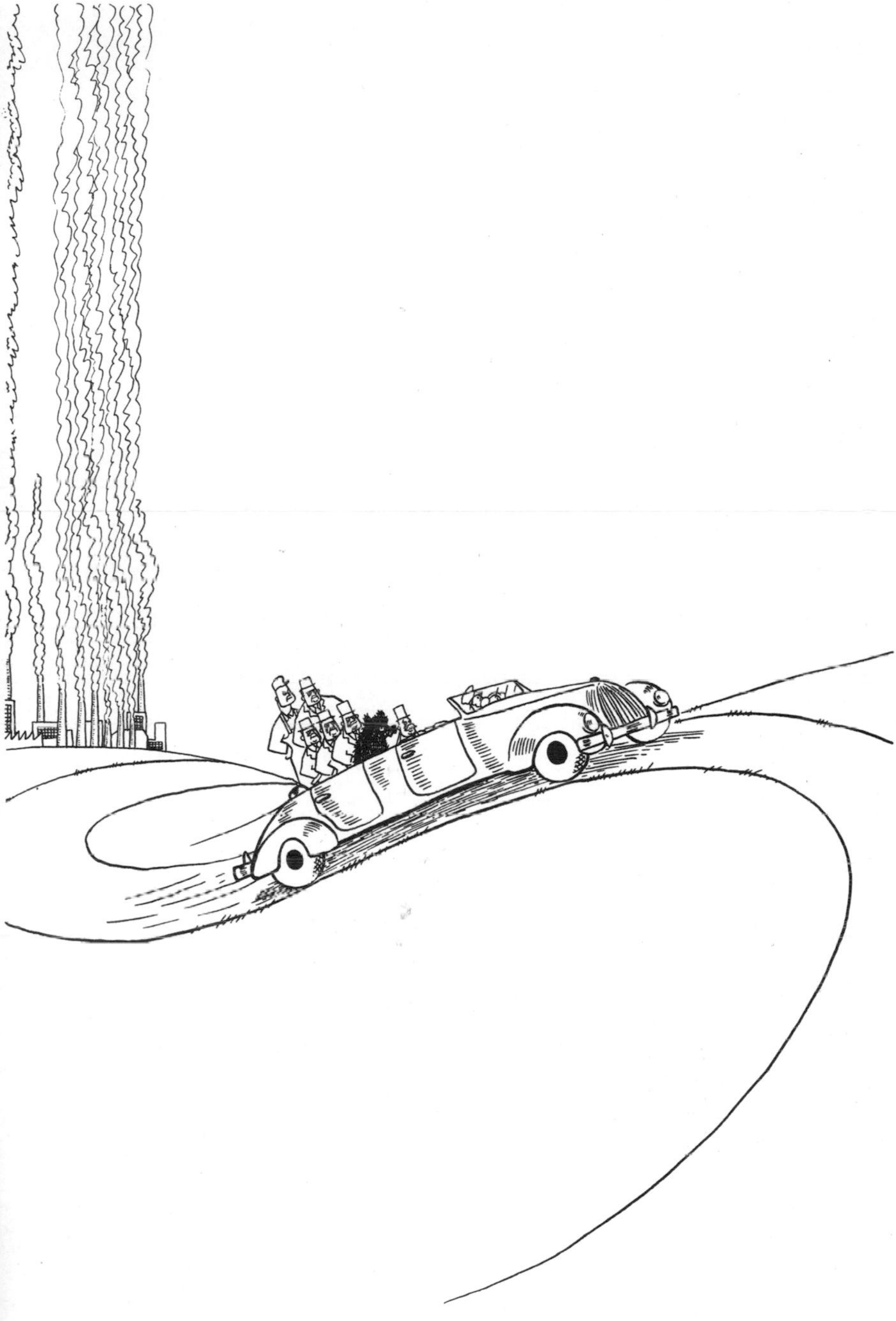

"Is he a *Bear?*" the President asked the zoo Bears.

The zoo Bears said, "No, he isn't a Bear, because if he were a Bear, he wouldn't be outside the cage with you. He would be inside the cage with us."

The Bear said, "But I am a Bear."

A little baby zoo Bear said, "I know what he is. He's a
silly man who needs a shave and wears a fur coat."

All the zoo Bears laughed.

The Bear said, "But I am a Bear."

AND

SO

THEY

ALL

LEFT

THE

ZOO

AND

DROVE

SIX

HUNDRED

MILES

AWAY

TO

THE

NEAREST

CIRCUS

"Is he a *Bear?*" the President asked the circus Bears.

The circus Bears said, "No, he isn't a Bear, because if he were a Bear, he wouldn't be sitting in a grandstand seat with you. He would be wearing a little hat with a striped ribbon on it, holding on to a balloon and riding a bicycle with us."   The Bear said, "But I am a Bear."

One little baby circus Bear said, "I know what he is. He's a silly man who needs a shave and wears a fur coat."

All the circus Bears almost fell off their bicycles laughing.

The Bear said, "But I am a Bear."

They left the circus and drove
back to the factory.

And so they put the Bear to work on a big machine with a lot of other men. The Bear worked on the big machine for many, many months.

One day a long time afterward, the factory closed down
and all the workers left and went home.
The Bear walked along far behind them. He was all
alone, and had no place to go.

As he walked along,
he happened to gaze up
at the sky. Away up high,
he saw a flock of geese flying
south.

Then the Bear gazed up at the trees. The leaves had turned
all yellow and brown and were falling from the branches.

The Bear knew when the geese flew south and the leaves fell from the trees, that winter would soon be here and snow would cover the forest. It was time to go into a cave and hibernate.

So he walked over to a huge tree that had a cave hollowed
out beneath its roots. He was just about to go into it,
when he stopped and said,

"But I **CAN'T** go into a cave and hibernate.

I'm **NOT** a Bear. I'm a silly man who needs a shave
and wears a fur coat."

So winter came. The snow fell. It covered the forest and it covered him. He sat there, shivering with cold and he said, "But I sure wish I was a Bear."

The longer he sat there the colder he became. His toes were freezing, his ears were freezing and his teeth were chattering. Icicles covered his nose and chin. He had been told so often, that he was a silly man who needed a shave and wore a fur coat, that he felt it must be true.

So he just sat there, because he didn't know what a silly man who needed a shave and wore a fur coat would do, if he were freezing to death in the snow. The poor Bear was very lonely and very sad. He didn't know what to think.

Then suddenly he got up and walked through the deep snow toward the cave.

Inside, it was cosy and snug. The icy wind and cold, cold snow couldn't reach him here. He felt warm all over.

He sank down on a bed of pine boughs and soon he was
happily asleep and dreaming sweet dreams, just like all
bears do, when they hibernate.
So even though the

FOREMAN
and the
GENERAL MANAGER
and the
THIRD VICE-PRESIDENT
and the
SECOND VICE-PRESIDENT
and the

FIRST
VICE-PRESIDENT
and the
PRESIDENT
and the
ZOO BEARS
and the
CIRCUS BEARS

had said, he was a silly man who needed a shave and wore
a fur coat, I don't think he really believed it, do you?
No, indeed, he knew he wasn't a silly man,

and he wasn't a silly Bear either.

DOVER BOOKS
FOR YOUNG AND OLD

Fables in Slang, More Fables in Slang, George Ade. $1.00

The Wonderful Wizard of Oz, L. Frank Baum. $1.50

The Marvelous Land of Oz, L. Frank Baum. $1.50

The Bad Child's Book of Beasts, More Beasts for Worse Children, A Moral Alphabet, Hilaire Belloc. $1.00

The Cruise of the Cachalot, Frank T. Bullen. $1.00

The Purple Cow and Other Nonsense, Gelett Burgess. $1.00

Three Martian Novels: Thuvia, Maid of Mars; The Chessmen of Mars; The Master Mind of Mars, Edgar Rice Burroughs. $1.85

The Land That Time Forgot, The Moon Maid, Edgar Rice Burroughs. $2.00

Pirates of Venus, Lost on Venus, Edgar Rice Burroughs. $1.75

At the Earth's Core, Pellucidar, Tanar of Pellucidar: Three Science Fiction Novels, Edgar Rice Burroughs. $2.00

A Princess of Mars, Fighting Man of Mars, Edgar Rice Burroughs. $1.75

Five Great Dog Novels, edited by Blanche Cirker (The Call of the Wild, Jack London; Rab and His Friends, John Brown; Bob, Son of Battle, Alfred Ollivant; Beautiful Joe, Marshall Saunders; A Dog of Flanders, Ouida). $1.75

The Brownies: Their Book, Palmer Cox. $1.50

Mr. Dooley on Ivrything and Ivrybody, Finley Peter Dunne. $1.00

Household Stories by the Brothers Grimm. $1.35

She, Allan Quatermain, King Solomon's Mines: Three Adventure Novels, H. Rider Haggard. $2.00

The Peterkin Papers, Lucretia P. Hale. $1.00

The Prisoner of Zenda, Rupert of Hentzau, Anthony Hope. $1.35

The Complete Nonsense of Edward Lear. $1.00

The Circus from Rome to Ringling, Earl Chapin May. $2.00

Paper Folding for Beginners, William D. Murray and Francis J. Rigney. $1.00

Topsys and Turvys, Peter S. Newell. $1.00

Peck's Bad Boy and His Pa, George W. Peck. $1.35

Singular Travels, Campaigns, and Adventures of Baron Munchausen, Rudolph E. Raspe. $1.00

Sailing Alone Around the World, Capt. Joshua Slocum. $1.00

The Casting Away of Mrs. Lecks and Mrs. Aleshine, Frank Stockton. $1.25

The Time Stream, The Greatest Adventure, The Purple Sapphire: Three Science Fiction Novels, John Taine (Eric Temple Bell). $2.00

Two Little Savages, Ernest Thompson Seton. $1.75

From the Earth to the Moon, All Around the Moon, Jules Verne. $1.75

To the Sun?, Off on a Comet!, Jules Verne. $1.75

A Nonsense Anthology, Carolyn Wells. $1.35

A Whimsey Anthology, Carolyn Wells. $1.25

Three Prophetic Novels (The Time Machine, A Story of the Days to Come, When the Sleeper Wakes), H. G. Wells. $1.50

Seven Science Fiction Novels (The War of the Worlds, First Men in the Moon, The Time Machine, In the Days of the Comet, The Food of the Gods, The Invisible Man, The Island of Dr. Moreau), H. G. Wells. Clothbound $4.50

Twenty-Eight Science Fiction Stories, H. G. Wells. Clothbound $4.50

The War in the Air, In the Days of the Comet, The Food of the Gods, H. G. Wells. $2.00

David Harum, Edward N. Westcott. $1.15

How to Tell the Birds from the Flowers, Robert W. Wood. 75c

Ding Dong Dell: A First Book of Nursery Songs, Percy M. Young and Edward Ardizzone. Clothbound $3.50